Forest,
What Would You Like?

by **Irene O'Garden**

illustrated by **Pat Schories**

Holiday House / New York

Forest, what would you like?

I would like you to visit me and linger.
I would like sun, Summer sun!
Sun for plants to grow—sun, flowers, trees, plants.
Trees! Plants! Water.
I would like some glistening leaves.

Forest, what would you like?

I would like clover and raspberry bushes,
caterpillars, butterflies! Turtles, newts,
and tadpoles, thumb-size mice.
I would like a slug.
Vines for animals to swing on.
Kits and cubs tumbling! I would like to laugh.

Forest, what would you like?

I would like friendship, fruit, song,
and all the spicy smells of Fall:
acorns, seeds, and crispy needles.
I would like my leaves to turn different colors
and a whole bunch of birds to fly through me.

Forest, what would you like?

I would like soaring hawks and the harvest moon.
I would like open spaces for people to lie down
to look at the stars at night.
Peace. Peace.
Peace.

Forest, what would you like?

I would like snow in Winter.
An icy river and a crystal rock,
a rock with a fossil,
a rock to rest on.
Rocks.
Breath of silver fox.

Forest, what would you like?

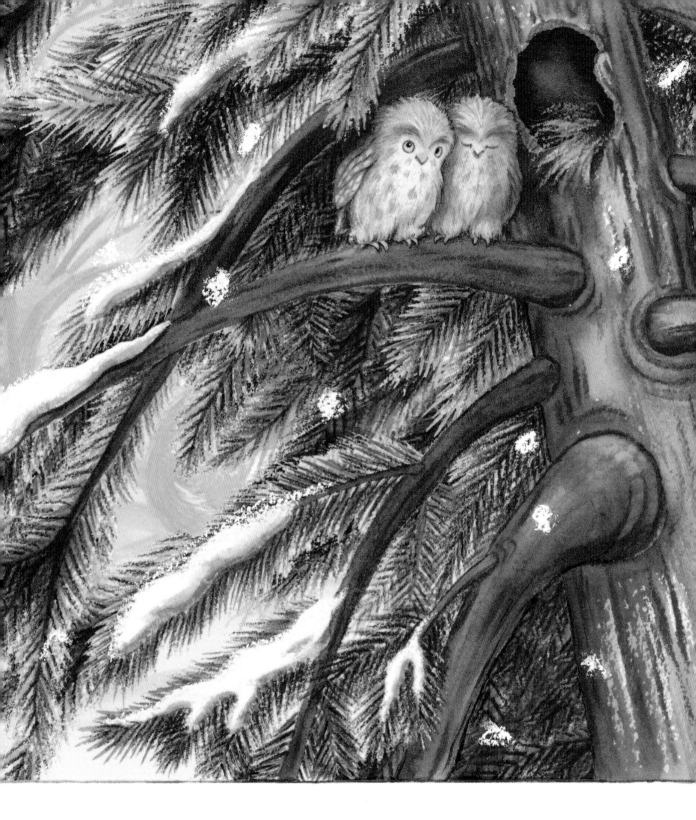

I would like thickets for my deer,
burrows for my furry ones,
deep-green fir tree wings
to hide my tiny owls.
And later, maple sugar.

Forest, what would you like?

I would like rain in Spring.
Breezes off the melting river.
More moss. Bees buzzing.
Flowers everywhere.
I would like moist soil.
Black birch trees that smell like root beer.

Forest, what would you like?

Tender feet. Cleaner trails.
People planting trees.
Love, love, love.

Forest, what would you like?

I would like Children,
always Children,
ever Children,
rambling my soils and rocks and limbs and moss,
always Children sniffing my flowers,

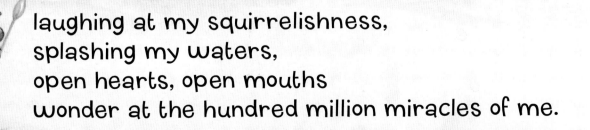

laughing at my squirrelishness,
splashing my waters,
open hearts, open mouths
wonder at the hundred million miracles of me.

I would like you to visit.
Often. And linger.

Author's Note

One June day, I was asked to participate in a
celebration of the Garrison School Forest with
four hundred children from the Garrison Union
Free School in Garrison, New York. Gowned as
Mother Nature, I asked each child to tell me how
the forest might answer the question: Forest,
what would you like? From their four hundred
responses, to which I added answers of my own,
I distilled a ten-page poem, which is here further
distilled into picture book form.

To Jean Marzollo,
who bubbles with wisdom and warmth
—I. O.

Text copyright © 2013 by Irene O'Garden
Illustrations copyright © 2013 by Pat Schories
All Rights Reserved
HOLIDAY HOUSE is registered in the U.S. Patent and Trademark Office.
Printed and Bound in October 2012 at Kwong Fat Offset Printing Co. Ltd., DongGuan City, China.
The text typeface is Family Dog Regular.
The artwork was prepared with watercolor paints on Arches Cold Press paper. For each illustration, two paintings,
one for the foreground and one for the background, were created, then scanned and combined in Photoshop.
The composite was printed onto Arches Cold Press paper, which was overpainted with watercolors.
www.holidayhouse.com
First Edition
1 3 5 7 9 10 8 6 4 2

Library of Congress Cataloging-in-Publication Data
O'Garden, Irene.
Forest, what would you like? / by Irene O'Garden ; illustrated by Pat Schories. - 1st ed.
p. cm.
Summary: A forest details the things that would make it happy such as sun, flowers,
trees, water, animals, and children rambling, climbing, and playing.
ISBN 978-0-8234-2322-4 (hardcover)
[1. Forests and forestry—Fiction. 2. Forest ecology—Fiction. 3. Nature—Fiction.] I. Schories, Pat, ill. II. Title.
PZ7.O33135Fo 2013
[E]—dc23
2011014900